THERE'S A
CROCODILE
UNDER MY BED!

A Red Fox Book
Published by Random House Children's Books
20 Vauxhall Bridge Road, London SW1V 2SA
A division of The Random House Group Ltd
London Melbourne Sydney Auckland
Johannesburg and agencies throughout the world

1 3 5 7 9 10 8 6 4 2

First published in Great Britain by Hutchinson Junior Books 1980
Red Fox edition 2000

Printed in Singapore by Tien Wah Press (PTE) Ltd

THE RANDOM HOUSE GROUP Ltd Reg. No. 954009
www.randomhouse.co.uk

There's a
Crocodile
Under my Bed!

Ingrid and Dieter Schubert

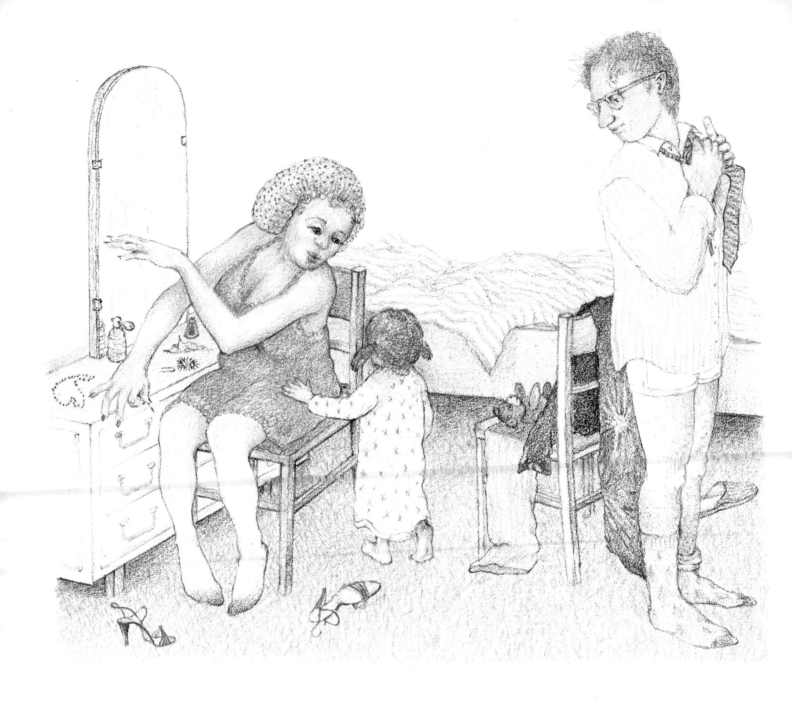

'Time for bed, Peggy,' says Dad.
    Mum and Dad are going out, so there's no time for
a story tonight.

Peggy skips along the corridor to her room, opens the door
and . . . Oh! There is a CROCODILE hiding under her bed,
his eyes shining yellow in the dark.

'I can't go to sleep!' Peggy yells to her parents. 'There's a crocodile under my bed!'

'Oh Peggy,' sighs Mum, 'we haven't got time for games now.'

'Show me,' says Dad. He switches on the light in her room, and they look under the bed.

'No crocodile,' says Dad. 'Just shoes and toys and a lot of old rubbish. Now go to sleep, Peggy. Grandma's here, but don't call her unless you have to.'

He tucks her in, turns out the light and leaves the room.

Peggy hears someone giggling. She looks under the bed – no-one there. And no-one behind the curtains.

'Up here!'

A huge crocodile is grinning at Peggy from the top of the wardrobe.

'I'm Henry,' he says, jumping down.

Peggy says nothing. She just clutches her bear and stares, round-eyed.

'You're not scared, are you?' says Henry.
'I'm very friendly.' He begins to shrink,
getting smaller and smaller until he
could fit into Peggy's shoe. 'Do you like
me better this size?' he asks.

Peggy thinks for a minute, then
smiles at him. 'I prefer you big,' she says,
'so we can play with each other.'

In a few seconds, Henry is his
normal size again.

'What shall we play first?' asks Peggy.

But Henry is covered with dust from the top of the wardrobe. 'I would like to wash first,' he says.

So Peggy runs a bath, with lots of Mum's bubble bath, and Henry jumps in. 'Come and join me,' he cries. 'It's lovely and warm.'

Peggy is a seamonster,
threatening the boats and
tipping the dolls in the water.
Henry rescues them with his
tail, swishing them over the
side to safety.

The water is getting cold. Peggy and Henry play a while longer,
then they dry themselves and go downstairs.

'Let's have some music,' says Henry. 'I will teach you
the Crocodile Rock.'

Peggy turns on the radio, and away they go.

The Crocodile Rock is great! They dance until they have
no breath left.

'You're the best crocodile dancer ever,' says Peggy,
panting.

'Now what shall we do?' asks Peggy.
    'Let's make a crocodile,' says
Henry. 'A tiny one.'

'We need two egg-boxes,' says Henry,
'one bigger than the other if
possible. We need green paint and
red paint and paint brushes. We need
white paper and scissors and glue,
and a piece of string.'

They glue the big egg-box so it
stays shut, and that makes the body.
They paint the small egg-box red
inside, and stick in sharp pointy
teeth cut out of white paper. That
makes the head. They fix a paper
tail to one end of the body, and tie
the head to the other, then they
paint the crocodile green outside,
with two fierce eyes.

'He looks much more frightening
than you, Henry,' giggles Peggy.

Peggy is beginning to yawn, so Henry carries her to bed.

'I'll tell you a story,' he says, 'about me when I
was little.

I lived in the Land of Crocodiles, which is sunny and
beautiful and far away. Many animals lived there – elephants
and ostriches and hippopotamuses and tortoises and, of course,
crocodiles.'

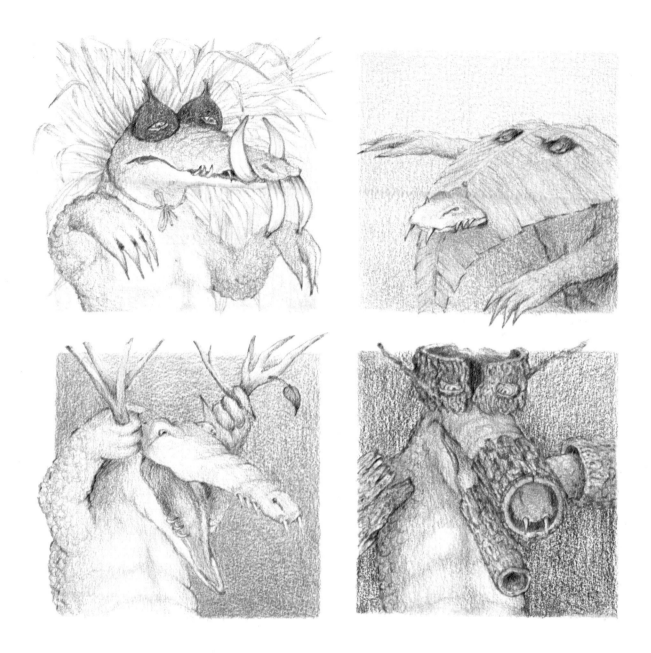

'I was very naughty, and I used to tease the small animals.
I told them scary stories about ghosts and witches. I dressed
up as a monster to frighten them. Once I rose out of the
river with long seaweed hair, and they all ran away.'

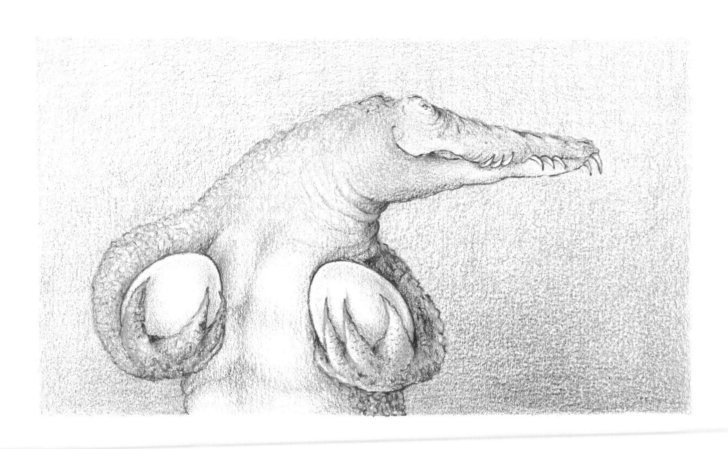

'Then I had a very wicked idea. I swopped the ostriches'
eggs with the crocodiles' eggs. When they hatched out,
their parents were furious.'

'The crocodiles' babies had feathers and beaks. The ostriches' babies had scaly skins, and wanted to swim in the river.'

'I was in terrible trouble.

I was called before the Council
of Seven Wise Crocodiles, and everyone
complained about me. The eldest
of the Wise Crocodiles told me what
they had decided to do.

"You have behaved very badly,"
he said. "You have scared the small
animals and upset their parents.
This must stop.

We are sending you away to the
Land of Men. Many children there
are afraid – of the dark, perhaps,
or of bad dreams. You must learn to
comfort them, and teach them there
is nothing to fear. Will you try?"
I promised I would.

"To help you, we will give you
two gifts: you will be able to speak
the language of men, and to make
yourself tiny so as not to scare
anyone. When you have visited a
thousand children, you can come
back to the Land of Crocodiles."'

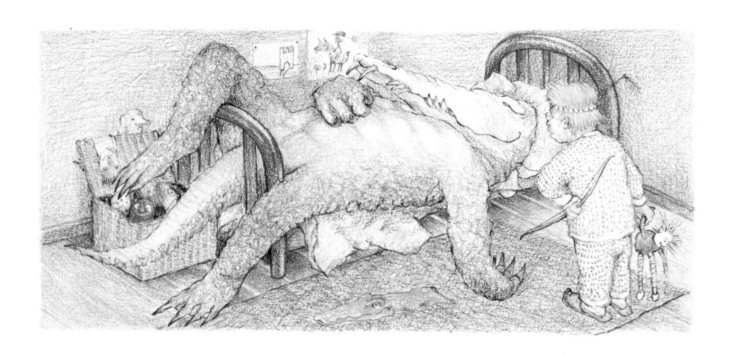

'The wise old crocodile gave me a drink which sent me to
sleep, and when I woke up I was in a little boy's room – in
fact, I was lying in his bed! We had great fun playing
Cowboys and Indians together.

   You, Peggy, are the seven hundred and seventy sixth
child I have visited. One day . . .'

   Henry stops, for Peggy is asleep.

Gently he tucks her in, turns out the light
and leaves the room.

'Hello Peggy,' says Mum next morning. She opens the curtains,
letting in bright sunshine.

　'Look,' says Dad, laughing. 'There *was* a crocodile
under your bed, Peggy. An egg-box crocodile!'

　Peggy just smiles.